It was unusually quiet at Hilltop Hospital.

Dr Matthews was having a cup of tea with Staff Nurse Kitty.
'Raining cats and dogs,' he said, looking out of the window.
Then he added, 'Oh, oh. Trouble.'

HILLTOP HOSPITAL

Nicholas Allan

RED FOX

To Millie

A Red Fox Book

Published by Random House Children's Books
20 Vauxhall Bridge Road, London SW1V 2SA

A division of Random House UK Ltd
London Melbourne Sydney Auckland
Johannesburg and agencies throughout the world

© Nicholas Allan 1992

First published by Hutchinson Children's Books 1992

Red Fox edition 1994

Printed in China

RANDOM HOUSE UK Limited Reg. No. 954009

ISBN 0 09 910241 2

An ambulance swerved to a halt just outside the hospital, its blue light flickering in the rain. Out jumped Ted the driver and Ted his mate. They opened the doors and took out a stretcher.

It sagged like a hammock; they
could hardly carry it. Whatever was
under the blanket was very big and
very heavy.

As the two Teds staggered through the hospital doors, a grey trunk emerged from under the blanket and waved in the air.

'Oh, oh. It's Mrs Indianapolis,' said Dr Matthews.
'She must be ready to have her baby,' said Nurse Kitty.
They both hurried out of the staffroom.

'This way, Teds,' Nurse Kitty said, directing them towards the maternity ward.

'Be glad to put her down,' mumbled Ted irritably.

'Weighs as much as an ele - a hippopotamus,' mumbled the other Ted irritably.

They laid Mrs Indianapolis on the bed. Then Dr Matthews got out his stethoscope and listened to her stomach.

'How are you feeling, Mrs Indianapolis?'
    'Just about ready, Dr Matthews,' she
smiled.
    Dr Matthews knew Mrs Indianapolis well.
Ever since she had known she was going to
have a baby, Mrs Indianapolis had visited the
hospital regularly for checkups.

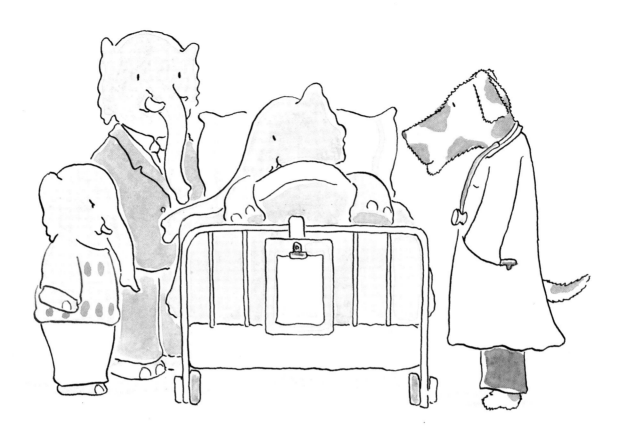

Nurse Kitty went to fetch the scanner so they could see the baby on the screen.

Just then Mr Indianapolis arrived with their son Virtue.

'Everything all right, Dr Matthews?' asked Mr Indianapolis.

'Yes, fine. Hallo, Virtue. I expect you're looking forward to having a little brother or sister.

Which would you like most?'

'*Neither!* 'Specially not a sister.' Then he kicked the bedframe.

'Now, now, Virtue,' Mr Indianapolis said, settling his trunk firmly on his son's shoulder. Virtue enjoyed being an only child and wanted to go on enjoying it. It made him feel sick to think he might have to share his life with a sister, or even a brother.

When Nurse Kitty came back with the scanner, Dr Matthews and she switched it on and inspected the screen.

'Looks rather a big baby,' said Dr Matthews.

'Yes, it does,' agreed Nurse Kitty, who always agreed with Dr Matthews, partly because he was usually right, mostly because she admired him.

'Even for an elephant,' he said. 'Better call Surgeon Sally.' He rang down to the theatre and Sally said she'd come right away.

When she arrived she was
dressed in her green smock
which tied up at the back,
and was taking off her
rubber gloves. She'd just
finished taking out Gertrude
the hyena's tonsils. Sally had
done four operations that
morning. She enjoyed her
work; Dr Matthews
sometimes wondered if she
enjoyed anything else.

Without saying a word,
Sally studied the screen.

'Caesarean,' she said at
once.

'Mm, looks like it,' agreed
Dr Matthews, who always
agreed with Surgeon Sally,
partly because she was
usually right, mostly
because he admired her.

'I'll prepare the theatre,' said Surgeon Sally.

Dr Matthews told Mrs Indianapolis that she must get ready to go down to the theatre too. The two Teds lifted her onto a trolley. Then they wheeled the trolley down the corridor. Mr and Mrs Indianapolis held trunks.

'Not nervous, are you, Mr Indianapolis?' asked Nurse Kitty.

'A bit,' he admitted.

'Not long now.'

'Well, we've waited twenty-one months, so we've learnt to be patient.'

When they reached the theatre doors Virtue had to say goodbye
to his mother. Nurse Kitty took him to the staffroom for an orange
juice.

'I expect you're *very* excited about having a little brother or sister. Which would you like most?' said Nurse Kitty.

'*Neither!*' said Virtue, ''Specially not a sister,' and almost kicked Nurse Kitty, but then thought about the orange juice.

In the theatre the nurses were

sterilizing the instruments.

Dr Atticus the anaesthetist was making preparations too.

'Now, let's see. Um, 20 mls Bupivacain with Adrenalin, 10 units Syntocifon, 20 mls Ephedrine, 4 lettuce leaves please, Nurse.'

'Four lettuce leaves, Dr Atticus?'

'Yes,' he said. 'Missed lunch. Feeling a bit peckish.'

Surgeon Sally put on her white mask, and slipped on a new pair
of gloves. She was looking forward to getting down to work.
When everyone was ready the two Teds lifted Mrs Indianapolis
very carefully onto the operating table.

'Right, we're off,' said Ted.

'And I 'ope you lot won't be seeing us again today,' said the
other Ted.

Dr Matthews, Dr Atticus, and Surgeon Sally gathered together briefly for a final consultation. Then Dr Matthews left knowing his patient couldn't be in safer hands.

He wandered back to the staffroom thinking he'd *just* have time for a cup of tea before the afternoon ward round.

But when he got there he found Nurse Kitty standing on one foot, as if someone had just stamped on the other one. Someone *had* just stamped on the other one.

'You all right, Kitty?'

'Oh, Dr Matthews,' said Nurse Kitty. 'Virtue's run away.'

'Bother,' said Dr Matthews. 'I suppose we'd better go and find him.'

Meanwhile, in the theatre, Surgeon Sally was working hard. All you could hear was Mrs Indianapolis' breathing and the low voices of Sally and her team.

'Scalpel.'

'Scalpel.'

'Swab.'

'Check gas.'

'Checking gas.'

'Where's that swab?'

'Swab on its way.'

After a long time and much wiping of Surgeon Sally's brow, it finally happened. Something small and grey and soft, with a delicate trunk which swayed from side to side, appeared in the room. It was held up in Sally's capable paws. Sally cast a clinical eye over it. She studied its ears, its legs, its tail and the tiny buds of its tusks.

'Girl,' she pronounced simply.

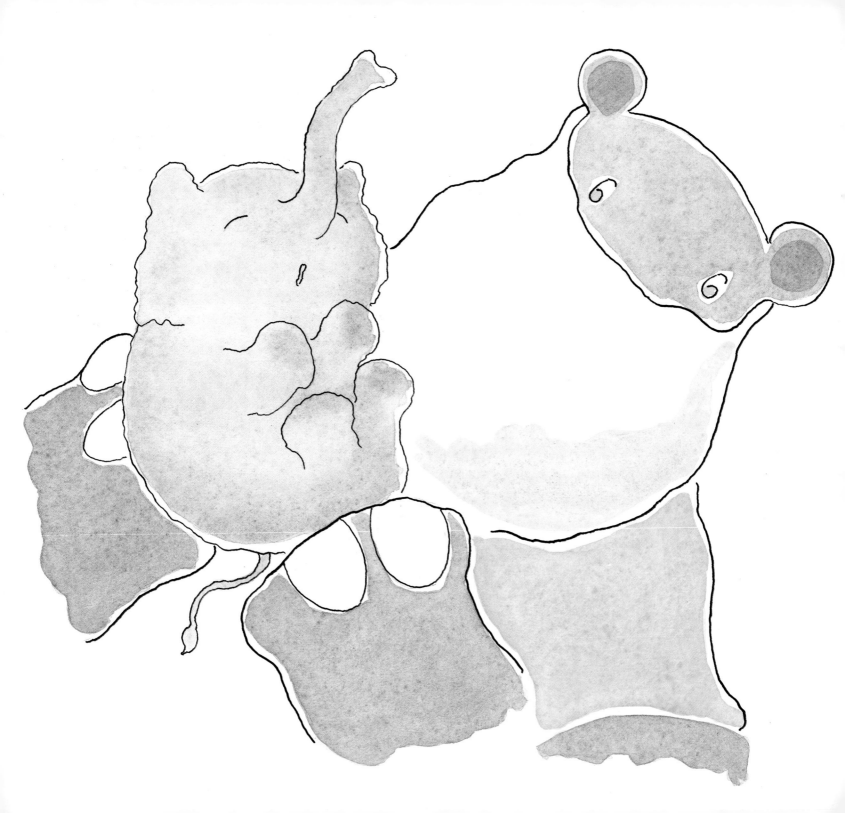

Then they washed her.

Then they weighed her.

Then they put her in a blanket.

And then they gave her back
to Mrs Indianapolis.
  'Oh,' said Mrs
Indianapolis, 'isn't she
lovely!'

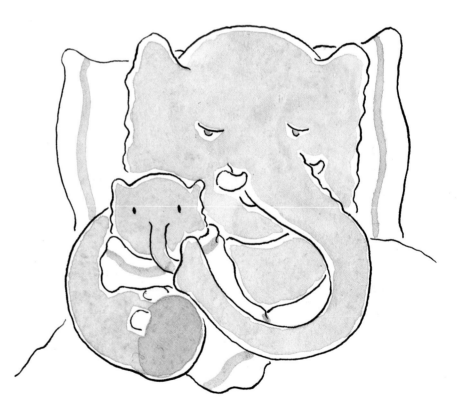

Meanwhile, Dr Matthews was still looking for Virtue. Virtue wandered down endless corridors – until he came to the laboratory.

He poked his head in and saw Clare and Arthur, the lab mice,
who were inspecting some blood samples.

'Hallo,' said Clare.

'My mummy's having a baby.'

'That's nice.'

'NO IT *ISN'T*,' he said, furious, and slammed the door. But now that he was lost and a little frightened, he became quite tearful. Dr Matthews and Nurse Kitty, however, had given up the search. They were on their way to the small ward where Mrs Indianapolis had been taken.

As they entered the room, they saw Mr Indianapolis sitting at the end of the bed beaming at his baby daughter snuggled up in his wife's arms.

'Isn't she lovely?' Mr Indianapolis clapped his paws with excitement. 'Just wait until Virtue sees her. Where *is* Virtue?'

'Ah,' said Dr Matthews wishing Mr Indianapolis hadn't asked.

'Ah,' said Nurse Kitty.

In fact, at that very moment, Virtue was trotting tearfully past the room where his mother lay. At that exact moment too, his baby sister cried out. Hearing his sister and recognizing the cry although he'd never heard it before, he turned, paused, listened, and finally rushed through the doors.

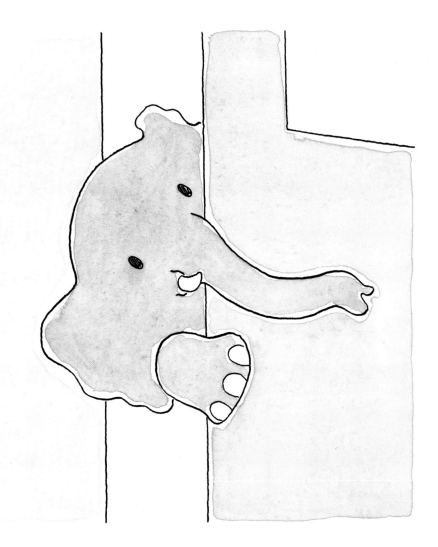

'Ah,' said Dr Matthews authoritatively.
'Ah,' said Nurse Kitty.

Virtue ran up to his mother with relief. Then he looked at the grey sleepy face of his sister. He looked at her with curiosity.

Only then did his sister stop crying and raise her tiny trunk. For a moment Virtue did nothing. But then, very gently, he raised his trunk too . . .

. . . until they touched.

'Ah,' everyone sighed.

And even Dr Matthews, that hardened professional, was not unmoved.

Several hours later, Dr Matthews and Nurse Kitty were sitting in the staffroom waiting for the tea to brew.

'Have you ever thought of having a family?' asked Nurse Kitty.

'Well, Kitty, I've always been too busy.'

'We're all busy, Dr Matthews. But you must relax sometimes.'

'I don't know if having a family's very relaxing,' said Dr Matthews, as he remembered Virtue, but he also thought how kind and friendly Kitty was being. Then he thought of Surgeon Sally and gazed dreamily out of the window. The rain had stopped; the sun had come out. But as he looked he suddenly said,

'Oh, oh. Trouble.'

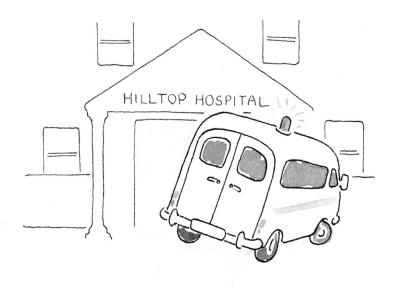

An ambulance swerved to a halt, its blue light flickering.

THE END